Turtellini
The Turbo-Charged Turtle

by Doug MacGregor

This is a book of fiction.
Names, characters, places and incidents either are the product of the author's imagination or are used fictitiously, and any resemblance to actual persons, living or dead, is entirely coincidental.

ISBN: 978-0-9654843-8-1
Library of Congress Control Number: 2011904862

Published by
Doug MacGregor
Fort Myers, FL
U.S.A.

This book is dedicated to those who wonder, imagine, and invent the future...

Turtellini thought
he was too slow.
He marveled at
the fishes
swimming about in
his neighborhood pond.
Boy, could they move!

Of course, Turtellini wasn't your average turtle. He was also a very clever inventor.

"I've got an idea!" he declared. "Monday, I'll go to my workshop and get busy!"

**Putting his brain to work,
he set out to be the
fastest turtle on water.**

"I know exactly
what to do," he said.

He got out his tools
and he drew right
through the night.

By morning, he had built a small engine from old parts in his workshop. He called it the Turtle Power One, or TP1 for short.

"This motor will make me the fastest turtle on water," he said.

He took the TP1 to Little Lost Pond behind his house, strapped it to his shell and launched it.

SPUTTER, SPUTTER,
SPLISH, SPLASH!!

"Holy spitfire sparks," he yelled. "I'm moving faster!" He motored around Little Lost Pond and suddenly realized he was running out of room.

“I need to go faster.
I’ll build a bigger engine
and find a bigger pond, too,”
he said to himself.

On Tuesday, he went back to his workshop.
He brought out more old spare parts.
He tinkered and toiled with a
new improved design.

After working all morning, he unveiled a *very fast* twelve-cylinder engine. He called it the VF12. It was much bigger than the TP1. He strapped it to his back and moved it to Higgins Lake. Higgins was a real lake and not some dinky little pond.

WHOMPER, WHIZZER, WHIRLEY, WHOOSH!

Now, this is faster for sure, he thought. Higgins Lake was a blur! Turtellini was plowing through the water like a big mouth bass. In less than five minutes, he circled the lake twenty times with the VF12.

"Now, I need a bigger lake and a bigger engine," he said.

On Wednesday, he went back to his shop and built a Turtle Turbo Prop 24 engine. It was twice as big as the VF12. He needed all the spare parts lying around the shop to build it.

Turtellini knew right where to launch his new invention.
He took it to Walloon Lake.
The TTP24 was so big
he needed a heavy
handcart to get it
there.

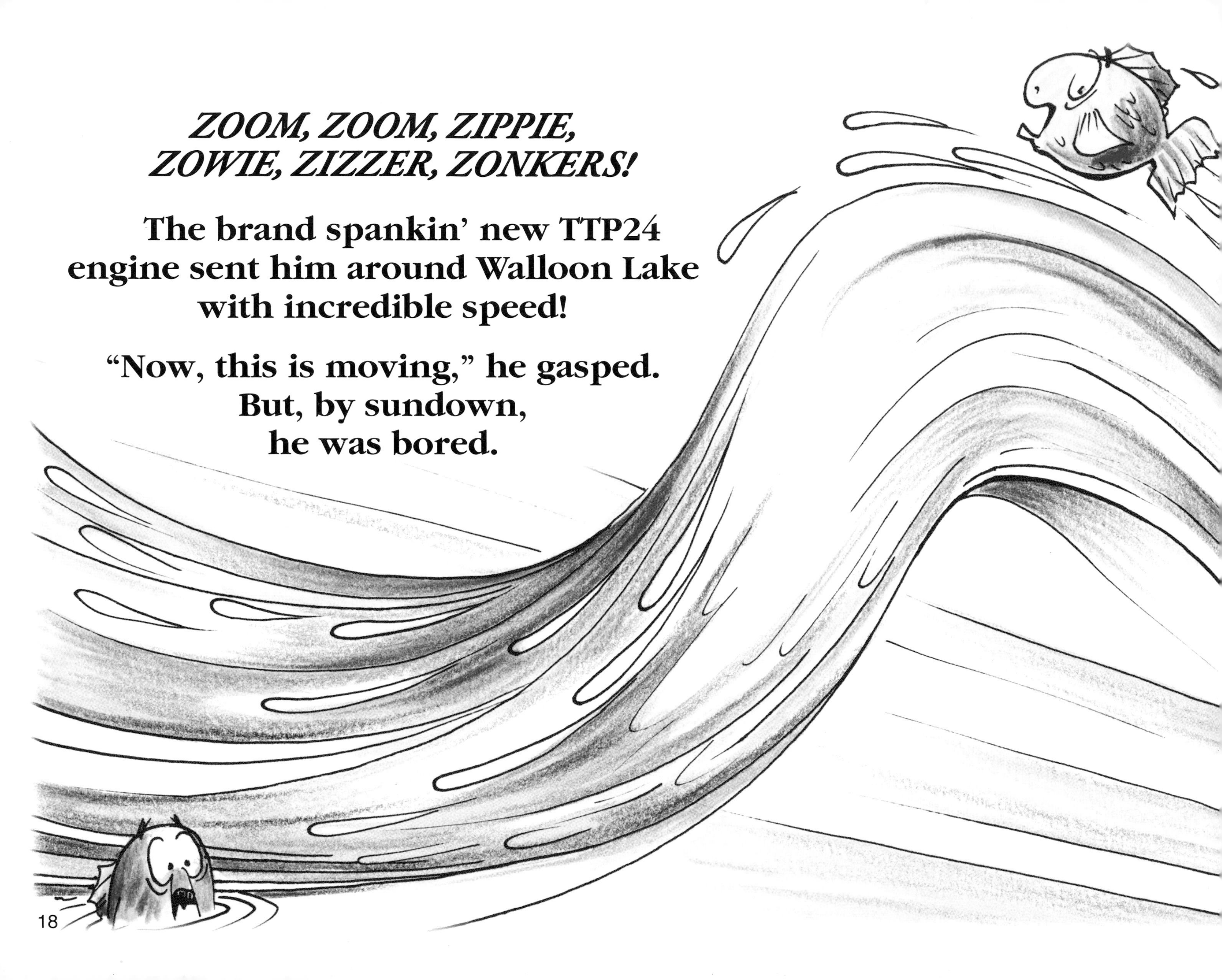

ZOOM, ZOOM, ZIPPIE,
ZOWIE, ZIZZER, ZONKERS!

The brand spankin' new TTP24 engine sent him around Walloon Lake with incredible speed!

"Now, this is moving," he gasped. But, by sundown, he was bored.

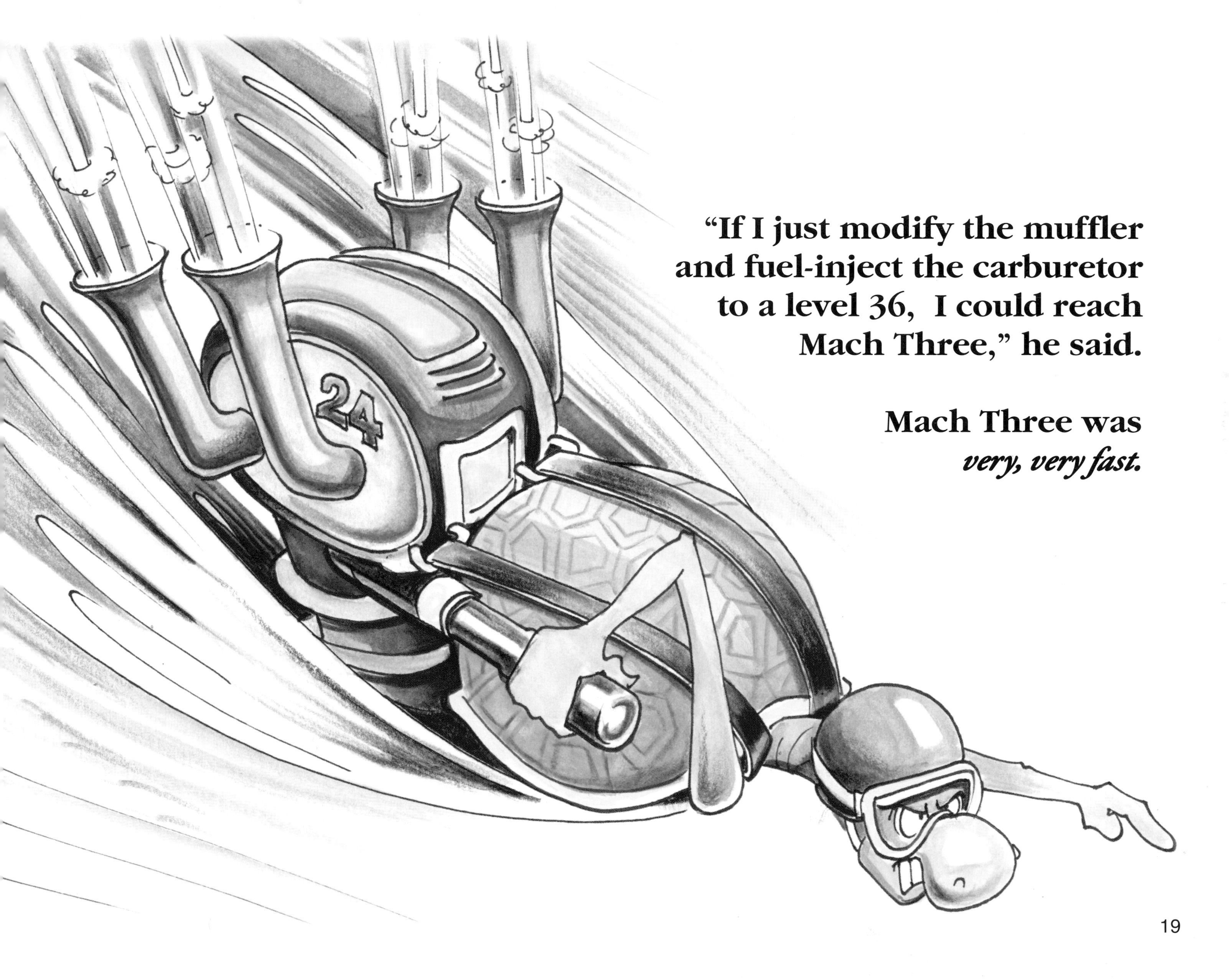

"If I just modify the muffler and fuel-inject the carburetor to a level 36, I could reach Mach Three," he said.

Mach Three was
very, very fast.

So back to the workshop he went,
with **bigger** ideas.

He worked on it
all night long.

Thursday morning he was tired,
but very excited to try out his latest invention.
The TTP36 engine weighed so much,
he needed to haul it in his wagon
to get it to the water's
edge.

Walloon Lake was now too small. He wheeled his new improved contraption two miles to Lake Humongous.

He bolted the beast of an engine to the stern of his shell and started it up.

RRRRUMBLE, RRRRUMBLE,
REVVVVV, REVVVV,
RRRUMBLE,
RRRUMBLE

A crowd had gathered on shore to watch the Great Turtellini launch the much improved TTP36. Wow!! No one had ever seen a motorized turtle before! No one had ever seen anything reach Mach Three speed! It was an historic day. The weather was clear, and the lake water was as smooth as glass.

With one twist of the throttle, The Great Turtellini zoomed off into the distance like a rocket! He reached Mach One in five seconds. He reached Mach Two in ten seconds. In twenty seconds, he was at Mach Three and gaining speed!

"This is incredible!" screamed The Great Turtellini.

The crowd was cheering and going crazy on shore, but The Great Tortellini couldn't hear them. All he could hear was the roar of his magnificent TTP36 engine!

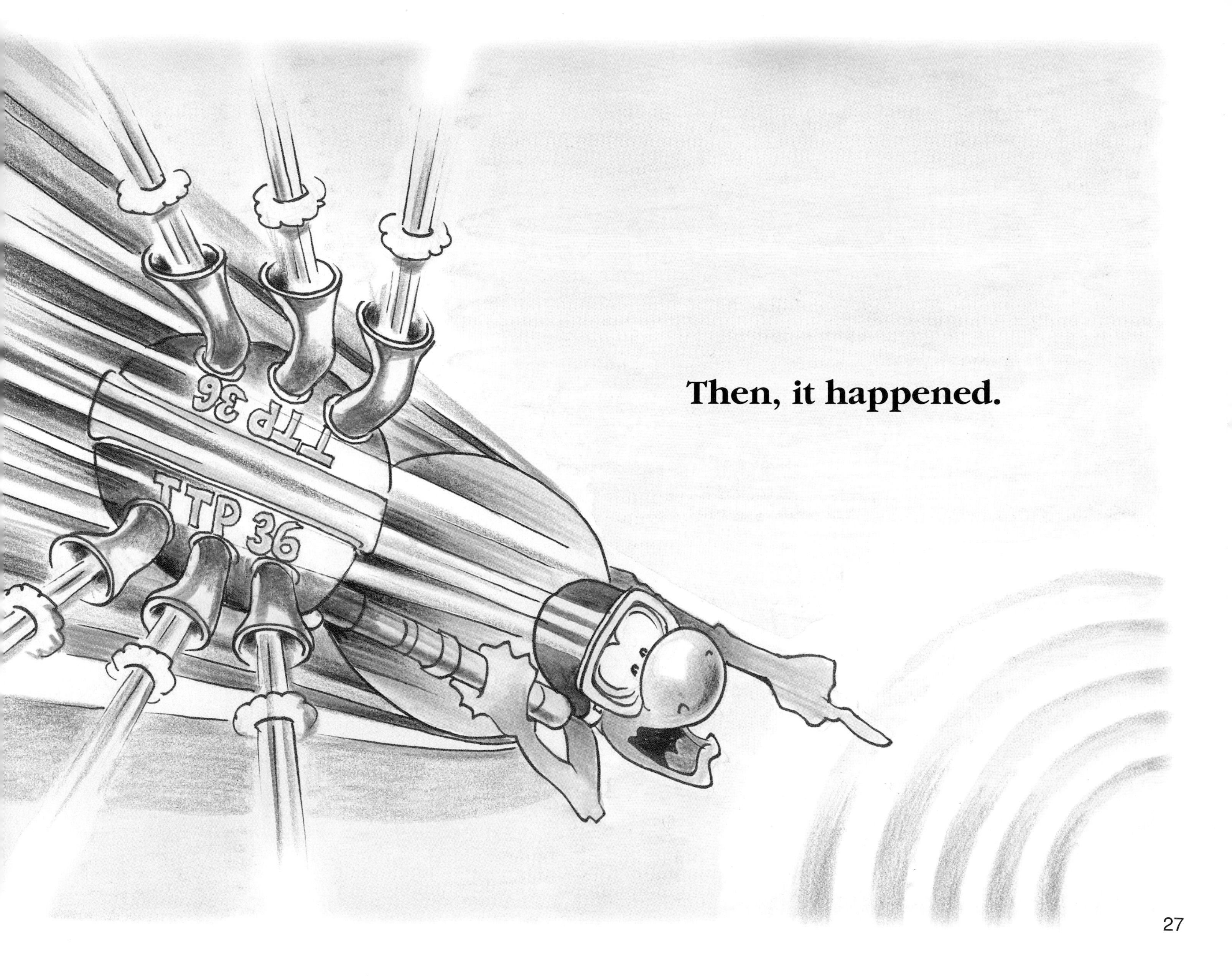

Then, it happened.

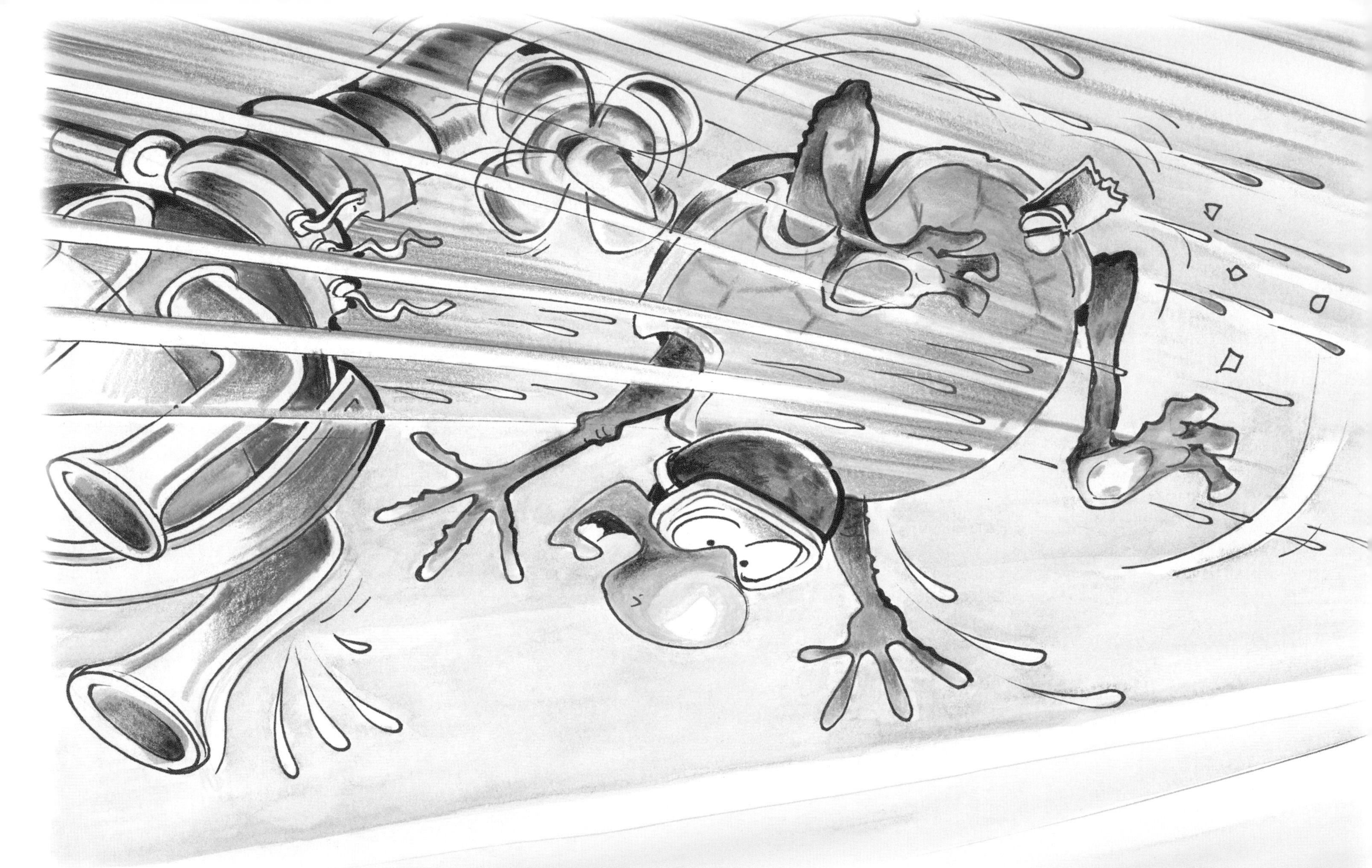

He hit a small ripple in the water, and before he knew it, he was airborne! The Great Turtellini was skimming across Lake Humongous like a wayward windsurfer.

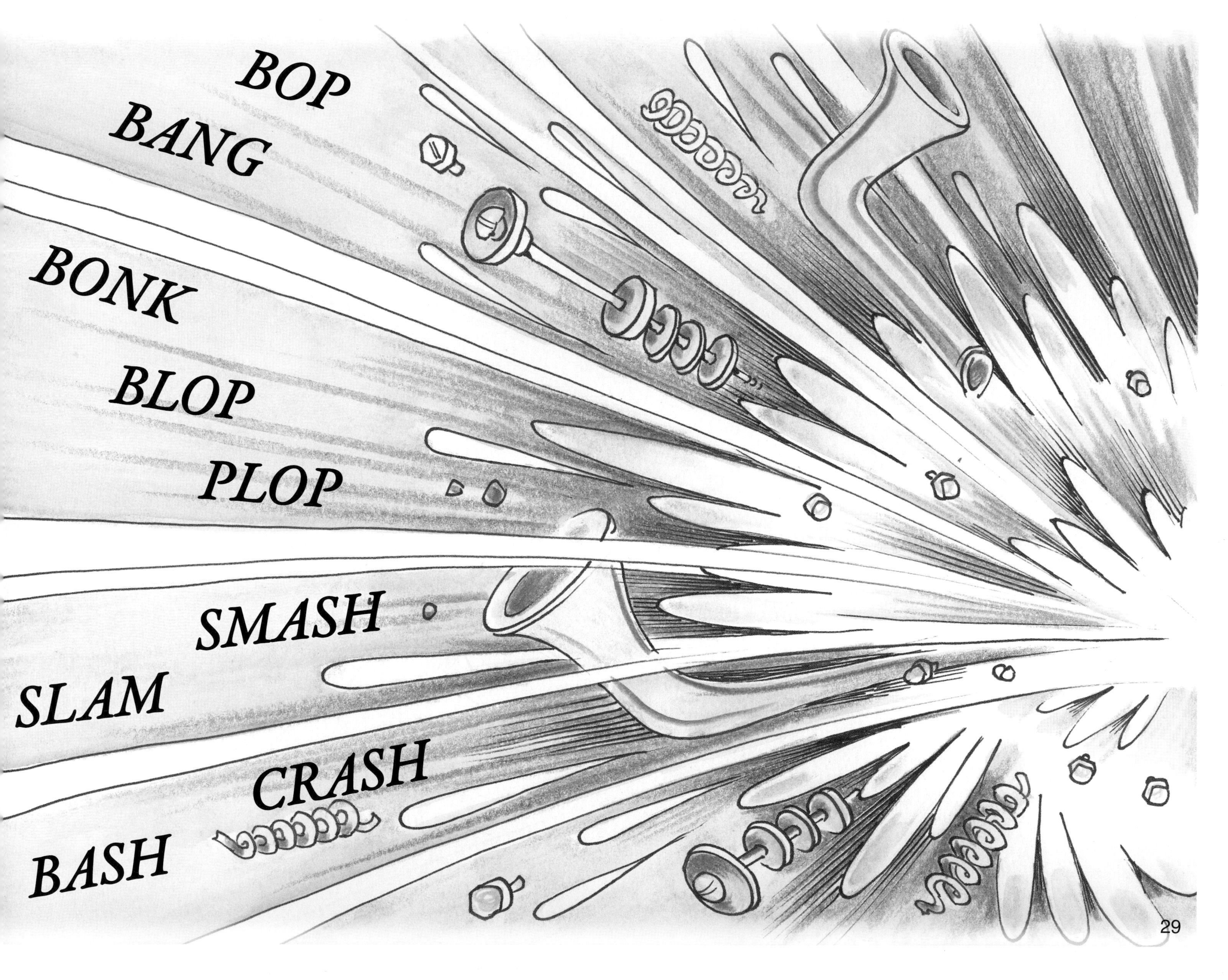
BOP
BANG
BONK
BLOP
PLOP
SMASH
SLAM
CRASH
BASH

The crowd was stunned! The Great Turtellini was knocked right out of his shell! He was nothing more than a soggy wet noodle now. His engine had smashed in a thousand pieces and was scattered all over Lake Humongous.

The Great Turtellini was very lucky. His favorite bike helmet and safety goggles had saved his life. He popped his humbled head out of the water and gave everyone the A-OK sign.

"Here, you'll need this," yelled a voice.

The lifeboat captain came to the rescue and gave
The Great Turtellini back his shell.
It was nicked up a bit, but was no worse for wear.

“That was quite a show, Mr. Turtellini. You were really flying!”

It was Friday morning. Turtellini woke up achy and stiff all over. He hobbled out of bed and walked outside to the driveway. He grabbed the morning newspaper and opened it.

Turtellini grinned from achy ear to achy ear.

Then, Turtellini looked up in the sky. He marveled at a lone seagull flying high above his sore head.

**Flight, he thought.
Hmmm...what would that
be like?**

He thought about it and thought about it.

That night,
all was quiet
in the
neighborhood
except for
one sound.

Crackle, crackle,
buzz, buzz.

Inside Turtellini's
lighted workshop,
sparks were flying.

It was four o'clock in
the morning.

At 6:45 am Saturday morning, his workshop doors flung open.

FLUTTER, FLUTTER, FLOOPH, FLOOPH, FLUTTER, FLUTTER

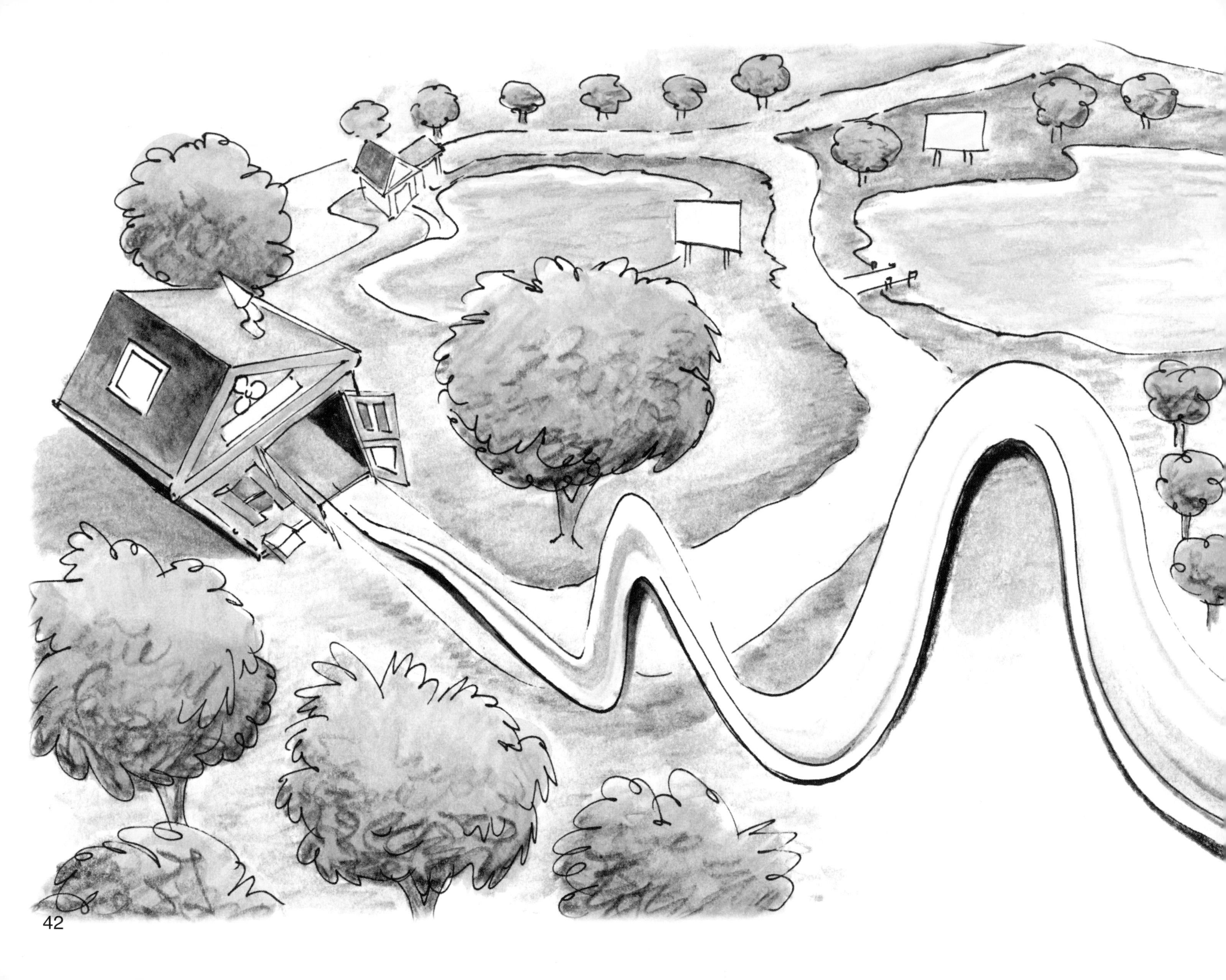

Yes, bigger ideas were reaching new heights.

The end.

Dare to dream like Turtellini.

Use the remaining pages to doodle, draw, design or invent something.

May all your design dreams come true.